Magic

Misty the
Scared Kitten

Bloomsbury Publishing, London, Oxford, New York, New Delhi and Sydney

First published in Great Britain in August 2016 by Bloomsbury Publishing Plc
50 Bedford Square, London WC1B 3DP

www.bloomsbury.com

A CIP catalogue record for this book is available from the British Library

ISBN 978 1 4088 7092 1

Typeset by RefineCatch Limited, Bungay, Suffolk
Printed and bound in Great Britain by CPI Group (UK) Ltd, Croydon CR0 4YY

1 3 5 7 9 10 8 6 4 2

Kitty's magic

Misty the Scared Kitten

Ella Moonheart

BLOOMSBURY

LONDON OXFORD NEW YORK NEW DELHI SYDNEY

Chapter 1

'Grandma! Grandma!' shouted Kitty Kimura excitedly. 'A postcard's arrived from Mum and Dad!'

Kitty ran to the kitchen. Emails were nice, but she loved getting post! The card had a picture of a waving ceramic cat on it. In Japan, they were a sign of good luck. Her parents were in Japan again now.

Grandma was pouring tea into her

flowery cup. She smiled as Kitty read the short message aloud and then stuck the postcard on the fridge.

Kitty's grandma had been born in Japan, but moved to England when Kitty's dad was little. Kitty's parents now owned a shop that sold special Japanese things, and Kitty loved all the silky kimonos, colourful fans and sparkly mobile phone charms. Three times a year, her parents went to Tokyo to look for new things for the shop.

Grandma lived with Kitty and her parents, so they spent lots of time together, especially when Mum and Dad were away. Kitty missed them, but she loved being with Grandma. They even looked alike, with the same

almond-shaped eyes. But Kitty's hair was long and black, while Grandma's bob had a streak of pure white on one side of her fringe.

'What shall we do for the rest of the week, Kitty-cat?' Grandma said.

Kitty's real name was Koemi, but

she loved cats so much that she was given the nickname Kitty, and now everyone called her that!

Just as Kitty was about to answer, the phone rang.

'I'll get it,' Kitty offered, running into the living room.

She picked up the phone. 'Hello?'

'Kitty!' said an eager voice. 'It's me, Jenny!'

Kitty was surprised. Jenny was her best friend, but they hardly ever phoned each other, because Jenny only lived three houses away. 'Hi!' she replied.

'Can you come to my house for a sleep-over tonight?' Jenny burst out. 'I have something really exciting to show you!'

Kitty giggled. Jenny was always

cheerful, but today she sounded even happier than usual. 'What is it?' she asked.

Jenny paused for a second. 'Well … I was going to keep it a surprise until you got here, but I can't wait. I've got a kitten!'

Kitty gasped. 'Jenny, you're so lucky!' she said, a smile spreading over her face. 'Why didn't you tell me before?'

'I didn't know until today!' Jenny explained. Kitty could hear her friend bouncing up and down excitedly. 'Mum kept it a surprise until I got home from school. My Auntie Megan is moving to America and she couldn't take her kitten with her – so she's given Misty to me! Wait till you see her, Kitty. She's gorgeous. She's pale grey with darker grey stripes. Mum says she's a silver tabby. And I think she likes me already. As soon as Auntie Megan brought her over, she ran straight up to me and rubbed herself all around my ankles!'

'I can't believe it,' Kitty said wistfully. 'I *love* cats.'

'I know! That's why I rang you straight away,' Jenny replied. 'It'll be as if she's your cat too! So can you come? We can play with Misty all evening!'

'Let me ask Grandma,' Kitty told her friend. 'I'll call you right back!'

She put down the phone and raced back into the kitchen. 'Grandma!' she called breathlessly. 'Can I sleep over at Jenny's house tonight? She's just got a *kitten*!'

Grandma put down her teacup. 'A kitten?' she replied slowly. 'Well, that's lovely for Jenny … but, Kitty, you know you start to sneeze as soon as you're anywhere near a cat.'

Kitty bit her lip. It was true. Ever since she was a baby she had been allergic to cats. It made her feel sad and a bit cross, because cats were her favourite animals in the whole world. She loved their bright eyes, their silky fur, and the soft rumble of their purring.

Most of all, she liked imagining what the cats in her village got up to at night, when people were fast asleep! What made it even harder was that cats seemed to really like *her*, too. They always followed her down the street, rubbing their soft heads against her ankles and miaowing eagerly. Kitty couldn't resist bending down to stroke them, but she always ended up with sore eyes and a runny nose.

'Oh, please, Grandma,' she begged. 'I'll take lots of tissues, and if I start to get itchy eyes or a tickly nose, I'll stop playing with Misty straight away, I promise.'

Grandma gazed thoughtfully at Kitty. 'Well, maybe you are old enough now,' she murmured softly, with the hint of a smile on her lips.

'What do you mean, Grandma?' asked Kitty, frowning. *Old enough that my allergy will be gone?* she thought, confused.

'Never mind,' Grandma told her, shaking her head. 'Wait here, sweetheart. I have something for you.'

Kitty bit her lip, curious. Grandma sometimes acted a bit strangely. She often took long naps at funny times, and she would stay up late, saying she was watching her favourite TV programmes. But now she was behaving even more oddly than normal.

When Grandma came back, she placed something carefully into Kitty's hands. It was a slim silver chain with a small charm hanging from it. At first Kitty thought there were Japanese symbols on it. But as she looked more closely, she saw it was a tiny picture of a cat.

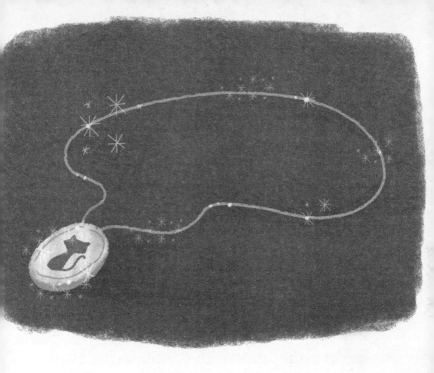

'Wow,' breathed Kitty, slipping the necklace over her head. 'It's beautiful.'

Grandma smiled and reached under her blue silk scarf to show Kitty a matching necklace. 'I have one too,' she explained. 'They have been in our family for a long time. Yours belonged to your great-grandmother. I've been keeping it safe until the right moment. It's very precious, and I know you will take good care of it. Make sure you wear it at Jenny's house. I think it will help with your allergies.'

'You mean ... I'm allowed to go?' cried Kitty. 'Thank you, Grandma!'

Kitty flung her arms around Grandma, though she was puzzled about what she'd said about the necklace. How could a piece of jewellery stop her from sneezing? But she was too excited to ask questions. She was going for a sleepover at her best friend's house, and she was going to play with a sweet little kitten!

Chapter 2

Half an hour later, Kitty and Grandma set off for Jenny's house, swinging Kitty's overnight bag between them. As soon as Kitty pressed the doorbell, the door burst open. Jenny's freckled face was flushed pink with excitement. 'I couldn't wait for you to get here!' she said with a grin. 'Quick – come and meet Misty!'

Jenny led them into the kitchen, where Jenny's mum and little brother Barney were painting. Jenny's mum washed her hands and made a cup of tea for Grandma. Kitty looked around eagerly for Misty. 'Where is she?'

'Over there, on the window sill!' said Jenny.

Kitty gasped as she spotted the little cat. 'Oh, she's *so cute!*' she cried.

Misty was curled cosily in a beam of warm sunshine. She was a soft grey colour, with darker grey stripes all over her body, and long silver whiskers. Her eyes were a pretty blue. When she spotted the girls, she sat straight up with pricked ears and gave a happy mew.

'She loves this sunny spot,' Jenny said, reaching out to pat Misty's head. 'Come and stroke her. She likes being tickled right here, between her ears.'

Grandma was watching out of the corner of her eye. Kitty touched Misty's soft, warm head gingerly, feeling excited butterflies fill her tummy. Misty closed her eyes and purred happily as Kitty stroked her all the way down to her long tail.

'She feels like silk,' whispered Kitty.

'I know. I love her so much. I still can't believe she's mine!' said Jenny, scooping Misty gently into her arms for a cuddle.

Kitty sighed. 'You're the luckiest girl in the world, Jenny. I wish I wasn't allergic to cats, then maybe Mum and Dad would let me have one too!'

Jenny raised her eyebrows. 'Oh gosh – I'd forgotten about that,' she said. 'Are you feeling all right at the moment?'

But before Kitty could answer, Jenny's mum came over. 'You're allergic, Kitty?' she asked worriedly. 'I didn't know that. Are you sure you'll be OK?'

Kitty nodded quickly. 'It's just a little tickle in my nose sometimes, that's all. I feel completely fine!' she said. Although at that very moment, she felt a twitch and her eyes began to tingle. She *really* wanted to rub them, but she ignored it. If Jenny's mum knew how bad her allergies could get,

Kitty knew she'd say they shouldn't have the sleepover. Even worse, she might never be able to stay at Jenny's house again!

'What do you think, Mrs Kimura?' asked Jenny's mum, turning to

Grandma. 'I've promised Jenny that Misty can sleep in her bedroom, but I don't want Kitty to feel poorly in the night.'

Kitty noticed Grandma glancing at the silver necklace. *Please don't change your mind now!* she thought desperately.

But to her relief, Grandma smiled. 'I think Kitty will be just fine,' she said.

'All right, then,' said Jenny's mum. 'No staying up late, though, girls. You know it's a special treat to have a sleep-over on a weeknight,' she added with a smile. 'I'll take both girls to school tomorrow, Mrs Kimura.'

Jenny and Kitty grinned at each other. Now they had the whole evening to play with Misty – and a little bit of tomorrow morning!

Grandma finished her cup of tea and thanked Jenny's mum. Kitty thought Grandma gave her an especially long, tight hug goodbye, but she wasn't sure why.

Once Grandma had left, Jenny said, 'Let's go to my room. I can show you all the special toys we've bought for Misty!'

They dashed up the stairs with Misty still curled up in Jenny's arms. She let Misty jump down on to the floor, and the beautiful tabby rubbed her pink nose against Jenny's leg, then started padding around, sniffing things.

'She explores by smelling everything,' Jenny explained. 'Auntie Megan said a cat's sense of smell is ten times better than ours! And they can see in the dark, and hear much better than us too.'

She picked up a squishy ball of pink wool and gave it a shake. Misty paused for a moment, her ears twitching. Then she leapt playfully at the ball, swiping it with her paw and knocking it from Jenny's hand. It rolled along the carpet, the wool unfurling as Misty chased it gleefully. Jenny and Kitty giggled. 'She's so cute!' Kitty said.

They played with Misty for the rest of the evening. Even when Jenny's mum called them for dinner, Misty followed the girls downstairs and padded around their feet as they

ate, looking up at them hopefully. Afterwards, they chose a film to watch in the living room. When they settled on the sofa, Misty hopped gracefully on to Kitty's lap, gave a friendly miaow and curled up in a fluffy ball.

'She really likes you!' Jenny told Kitty.

Kitty beamed and stroked Misty's velvety ears. She felt really lucky that Jenny was so nice about sharing Misty. And she felt even luckier that she had a new cat friend! The only problem was her allergies. She tried not to think about the strange itchiness in her nose and eyes, but the more time she spent with Misty, the worse it got. By the time the film finished, it was almost like her whole *body* felt odd!

Before she scrambled into her sleeping bag on Jenny's bedroom floor, Kitty pulled a packet of tissues out of her overnight bag and tucked them under her pillow. She hoped she wouldn't sneeze too much in the night.

Jenny dived into bed and Misty jumped on to the bedcovers to snuggle up by her feet.

'Sleep tight, girls!' called Jenny's mum, switching off the light.

'Goodnight, Kitty!' Jenny whispered happily. 'Today has been the best day ever!'

'I know! Night night,' Kitty whispered back. Before long, she was drifting into sleep.

Kitty's eyes flew open. It was very quiet in Jenny's bedroom. Moonlight was shining through a gap in the curtains. She knew straight away what had woken her up: her nose was tickling like crazy!

She rubbed it, but it didn't help. In fact, that only made it worse – now her cheeks were itching and her ears were tingling. Suddenly, Kitty noticed the tickly feeling was spreading. The tips of her fingers and toes felt like they were full of fizzy bubbles, and there was a strange prickling all over her arms and legs. Finally, she began to sneeze. 'Achoo! Achoo! *Aaaaa*choo!'

The bubbly, tickly feeling spread right through her and it felt like her whole body was sparkling and glowing. Kitty gave one more enormous sneeze. 'AAAAAAAACHOOOOO!'

When she opened her eyes again,

everything felt different. Her nose had stopped itching and her eyes weren't sore any more – but something was strange about them. *I must have got used to the darkness*, she thought. *I can see everything much more clearly!*

Then Kitty thought something else was odd. Jenny's bed was much bigger and further away. *How is that possible?* Kitty wondered. She looked around, and as her gaze drifted down, she stared in amazement. Where her hands had been before, there were now two small, furry black paws.

Cat paws.

Kitty cried out in shock – but the sound that came out wasn't a cry. It was a miaow.

Kitty's eyes widened as she realised what must have happened.

I don't know how, she thought, *but I think I've turned into a cat!*

Chapter 3

Kitty gazed down at her paws. She couldn't believe they belonged to her! Carefully, she lifted one up for a closer look. It was covered in soft black fur, with a white tip like a little sock. Underneath the paw were five tiny pink pads. *Is that really* my *paw?* she thought. *But how?*

Then Kitty had another thought.

Jenny. Was her friend awake? Glancing up at the bed, she saw that Jenny was still fast asleep. But next to Jenny's feet, Misty was sitting up and staring right at Kitty, her ears pricked up curiously. Quietly, she jumped down so that they were facing each other, nose to nose. This close, Kitty could see each beautiful fleck of gold in the tabby's blue eyes, even in the darkness.

Kitty heard her own name, whispered in a soft, friendly miaow. 'Kitty? Is that you?'

Kitty gasped. She could understand her! 'M-Misty? I've turned into a cat!' she stammered. To her surprise, the words came out as a miaow as well.

'How did you just change like that?' Misty asked.

'I don't know,' Kitty replied. 'One minute I'm sneezing, and the next I'm a cat!' Maybe she was dreaming!

'This is so exciting!' said Misty, her eyes bright.

Just then, Jenny yawned and turned over in bed. Both cats froze.

'Maybe we should go somewhere else to talk?' Kitty whispered.

'Follow me,' Misty replied.

She padded quickly out of Jenny's bedroom. Kitty hesitated, then followed Misty on to the dark landing and down the stairs. She took slow, careful steps at first, worried she might take a tumble. It felt so strange to be walking on four

unfamiliar paws instead of two feet –
and to feel her new tail swishing along
behind her!

In the kitchen, Misty trotted up to
the cat flap that Jenny's stepdad had
fixed in place that afternoon. She nimbly
dived through it, landing on the other
side with an excited little wriggle. The
flap swung shut again, and Kitty poked
her nose against it cautiously. She didn't
want to get stuck halfway! She pushed it
with her paw, then took a deep breath
and jumped. She managed to get through
in one go, but lost her balance as she
landed, and sprawled on the grass.

'Sorry, Kitty,' Misty giggled. 'I should
have held it open. This must be so strange
for you.'

'That's OK,' said Kitty, pulling herself back to all fours and looking around excitedly.

Jenny's back garden seemed like a different world: a moonlit jungle, full of exciting sounds, smells and places to explore. Kitty's cat eyes could see every blade of grass perfectly, and her sensitive ears could hear a mosquito buzzing at the other end of the garden! Looking around, she padded over to a puddle on the ground, shimmering in the moonlight like a mirror. She peered down at her reflection.

Instead of a small girl with dark hair, a little black cat stared back at her! Kitty gazed at her furry ears and the sprinkling of white whiskers on either side of her little black nose. All four of her paws were white and, as she curled her tail up into the air, she saw that had a white tip too.

And what was that around her neck? Kitty looked closer. It was the special necklace that Grandma had given her – but it had transformed into a collar! One thing was different, though: the picture of the cat had disappeared from the charm, and now there was the outline of a girl instead.

'This is all so weird,' Kitty said. 'I don't know what's happening to me!'

Behind her, Misty miaowed in agreement. 'I've never heard of a girl turning into a cat before!' she said. 'But I know who we can ask: the Cat Council.'

'What's that?' asked Kitty. *This dream is getting stranger by the moment!* she thought. *But I guess I'm just going to have to go with it until I wake up — or turn back into a girl!*

'There's a Cat Council in every

town. It's where all the local cats meet to talk and help each other with problems,' explained Misty. 'I can't wait to go to my first meeting here. The Council and their Guardian will help you. And apparently, this Council's Guardian is really special!' Her eyes were bright with excitement.

'What's a Guardian?' said Kitty. It sounded very impressive.

'Every Cat Council has an extra-wise cat who can help with any really serious cat problems,' Misty told her. 'I'm sure the Guardian will be able to help you, Kitty. Why don't we call a meeting for tomorrow night? It's done the same way everywhere, so all cats know what to do.'

'OK! So how do we do it?' asked Kitty.

'Watch!' said Misty. She padded up to the garden fence and scratched three claw marks on it, making a triangle shape, and rubbed her fur against the marking. She then made a long miaow that echoed into the night. Kitty's ears pricked up excitedly as she heard other cats miaow back in the distance.

'That's the sign that a cat needs help from the Cat Council,' explained Misty. 'If cats hear the signal, they check fences and lamp-posts for this special symbol! They'll be able to tell from the scent of my fur that I called the meeting.'

Kitty gave the post a sniff. To her surprise, she could make out Misty's unique scent.

'Wow,' she said. She had so many questions for the Cat Council already, even if she *was* dreaming all this! 'So cats can talk to each other?'

'Of course! Just like we are now. And cats can understand humans too,' Misty explained. 'So I could listen to you and Jenny chatting today.' Her blue eyes lit up. 'Jenny's great,' she purred happily. 'I'm so happy I get to play with her all the time! And I'm glad we're friends too, Kitty. It's going to be really fun having a human friend who can turn into a cat!'

Before Kitty knew what was

happening, Misty gave a mischievous miaow – and then pounced! Kitty squealed in surprise as she tumbled to the ground. As she and Misty rolled playfully in the grass, Kitty felt a warm, happy feeling in her tummy and then heard a low rumbling sound. She realised the sound was coming from *her*. 'I'm purring!' she gasped.

This was amazing! Kitty decided not to worry too much about whether this was a dream or not. She was just going to enjoy it while it lasted!

But unexpectedly, there was a soft *thump* and a low hissing sound behind them. Kitty and Misty spun around, and Kitty felt her ears prick up and her fur stand on end. In the shadow of the garden fence stood a large Persian cat with fluffy white fur, glaring at them through mean yellow eyes. Crouched on the fence was a second white Persian, with an expression just as nasty as the first. With another *thump,* he bounded down into the garden.

'You are on *our* territory,' hissed the first cat, flicking his tail.

'I'm Claws, and that's my twin brother, Fang. And guess what? This garden belongs to us,' said the other cat, baring his sharp teeth.

Kitty gulped. The garden felt very dark and dangerous all of a sudden, and these cats were big. Misty took a brave step forward and gave her friendliest miaow. 'I'm Misty, and this is Kitty,' she explained. 'It's nice to meet you. I just moved here today, so –'

Fang interrupted her rudely. 'We don't care who you are, New Cat,' he spat. 'All gardens around here belong to us now, including this one.

So you'd better scram! And if we see a *whisker* of you here again, you'll be dog food!'

'B-but this is where I live!' Misty protested, her eyes wide in alarm.

'We don't care!'

The Persian cats stepped closer, their eyes narrowed into cruel slits, and began prowling in a circle around Kitty and Misty, who huddled close together. Kitty felt her heart beating fast and noticed her back was starting to rise into an arch, the way she'd seen cats do when they were scared. 'What shall we do, Misty?' she whispered.

'Quick!' miaowed Misty. 'Run!'

She darted across the garden. Kitty didn't stop to think – she sprang past

the Persian cats and raced after Misty as fast as her new paws would carry her, just as the first cat swiped his sharp claws right where her head had been! There were angry snarls behind her, and Kitty glanced back to see Claws and Fang chasing after them. Quickly, she and Misty squeezed inside the thick hedge at the end of the garden. Misty backed away, but Kitty peered out of the leaves, panting hard. To her relief, the Persian cats stopped outside the hedge. Kitty heard them growling menacingly.

'You'll have to come out of there sometime,' she heard Fang snarl. 'And when you do, we're going to get you!'

Kitty turned to Misty. 'Shall we make a run for it?' she whispered.

'I'm not sure,' said Misty, looking very worried. 'We might be able to sneak out and run back to the cat flap before they notice – oh – what's that?'

She nodded at the ground by Kitty's front paws. Kitty looked down and saw something glinting in the moonlight. Her collar! It must have fallen off as she squeezed into the hedge.

Picking it up, she saw that some tiny words were etched on the back of the silver charm. Without even thinking, Kitty read them aloud.

'Kitten paws to human toes,
Kitten whiskers, human nose.'

Right at that moment, Claw lost his temper. 'Fine – I'm coming to get you!' he growled, and Kitty saw him crouching down as he got ready to pounce.

Suddenly, Kitty's nose began to tickle. Her tail itched and her paws twitched – and just as the Persian sprang into the hedge, everything around her went dark.

Chapter 4

'Girls! Time to get up!' called Jenny's mum.

Slowly, Kitty opened her eyes. The sun was streaming through the gap in her friend's bedroom curtains. Jenny was still cuddled up in bed with Misty curled by her feet and Kitty was safely in her sleeping bag. She reached for her necklace and saw that it was the tiny cat charm again – not a collar.

Kitty lay there for a moment, as the memories from last night flashed through her mind. She remembered the amazement she had felt as she looked down at her furry black paws ... being able to speak to Misty ... the nasty Persian cats in the garden ... and then, as she'd read the strange words on her collar, turning back into a girl. The Persians had been so shocked they had fled the garden as quickly as their paws could carry them. When she was sure they'd gone, Kitty had carried a trembling Misty back inside the house.

It had all *felt* so real, but ...

Kitty sat up and reached over to stroke Misty. 'Can you understand

me?' she whispered softly. But Misty just rubbed her head against Kitty's hand, purring.

Kitty felt a little bit relieved – and a little bit disappointed too. *It must have been a dream,* she told herself. *But it was the strangest, most magical dream I've ever had.*

Just then, Jenny stirred. 'Kitty,' she said sleepily. 'Were you talking to Misty?'

Kitty felt herself blush. 'I was only saying good morning,' she told her friend. 'Come on, let's get ready for school.'

By the time Grandma picked them up from school that afternoon, Kitty had almost forgotten about her funny dream.

'How was the sleepover, Kitty-cat?' asked Grandma, bending down to kiss her hello.

Kitty thought Grandma seemed nervous. *She must have been worried about my allergies*, she decided. 'It was fun, Grandma!' she reassured her. 'And I didn't sneeze much.'

Grandma nodded. 'That's good,' she said. 'Is there anything else you want to tell me?'

Kitty looked at Grandma, puzzled. 'Like what?' she asked.

'Oh, nothing,' said Grandma, shaking her head. 'Come along, girls.'

All the way home, they talked about Misty. 'Why don't you come in and play with her again for a bit, Kitty?' Jenny suggested as they walked down their street.

'Can I, Grandma?' asked Kitty hopefully.

'As long as it's all right with Jenny's mum,' agreed Grandma. 'And as long as you're home for tea!'

Once Jenny had checked it was OK,

Jenny and Kitty raced through the house, calling for Misty. 'I bet she's in that sunny spot by the kitchen window!' said Jenny — but Misty wasn't there.

'Maybe she's in the garden,' suggested Kitty. They went outside and looked around, peering under bushes and behind trees. Kitty got a funny feeling in her tummy as she looked under the hedge at the end of the garden. Even though she knew she had only dreamed about hiding inside it last night, it still *felt* real.

'Mum, we can't find Misty anywhere!' said Jenny as her mum came outside with two glasses of juice for them.

'Oh, I think she's in your bedroom,'

she replied. 'It's odd. She was settling in so well yesterday. She seemed to love the garden – she kept jumping through the cat flap with a funny little wriggle, as if she couldn't wait to get outside!'

Kitty almost dropped her glass of juice in surprise. *Misty did that in my dream!* she thought.

'But today, she hasn't been in the garden once,' Jenny's mum went on. 'She's jumped at every loud noise and hidden under the sofa. When I tried to encourage her to go outside, she bolted upstairs.'

Jenny looked worried. 'I hope nothing's happened to frighten her. Let's go and find her, Kitty.'

As the girls ran upstairs, Kitty's heart

was beating fast. *Was Misty afraid to go outside because of the Persian cats? Had it been real?* She needed to talk to Misty – alone!

The silver tabby was huddled on Jenny's bed, and gave a little miaow when Jenny and Kitty knelt down to stroke her.

'Let's try the ball of wool again!' said Jenny, rolling it across the floor – but Misty didn't seem to feel like playing today.

'Don't worry,' Kitty reassured Jenny. 'She's probably just tired. She had a busy day yesterday, meeting her new family!'

Jenny nodded, but Kitty could tell she was upset about Misty. 'Let's read your new *Animal Girl* magazine,' Kitty suggested, keen to take Jenny's mind off it.

They read the magazine together,
and were just filling in the puzzle section
when Jenny's mum called up, 'Can you
come down and set the table, Jenny?'

'I'll be back in a minute,' Jenny told Kitty. She nodded, her heart pounding. This was her chance! The moment she heard Jenny's footsteps thumping downstairs, Kitty turned to Misty and looked right into the tabby's blue eyes.

'Misty,' she said quietly, 'maybe I'm just imagining things ... but was last night real? Did I turn into a cat?'

She waited for a second, and felt her cheeks flush. She was going to feel so silly if this was all in her head! But to her amazement, Misty reached out a paw, placed it gently on Kitty's hand and miaowed emphatically.

'I *knew* it felt real!' gasped Kitty. 'And is the reason you haven't been

outside all day because of those horrible
cats, Fang and Claws?'

Misty gave a frightened little shiver.
Kitty stroked her head comfortingly –

and then remembered something else. 'The Cat Council!' she breathed. 'You called a meeting with them, for tonight. We can ask them what to do about those cats – as well as finding out why I can turn into one!'

Misty's little ears twitched and she glanced towards the door. Kitty listened, and heard Jenny coming back upstairs. 'Meet me in my garden tonight!' she whispered quickly. 'I live three houses away – it's the one with the oak tree and the Wendy house.' Misty tilted her head to one side, looking worried. Kitty stroked her reassuringly. 'It will be OK, Misty. Just make sure those nasty cats aren't around, then make a run for it.' The little cat looked up at Kitty and miaowed quickly in agreement.

As Jenny came back into the room, Kitty turned back to the word search they had been doing – but she could barely concentrate. Her whole body was tingling. What was going to happen tonight?

Chapter 5

Kitty was desperate for bedtime that evening. As soon as she and Grandma had eaten dinner, she raced upstairs and put her pyjamas on. Grandma chuckled when she saw them. 'Are you tired, sweetheart?' she asked, her eyes twinkling. 'Your sleepover must have worn you out!'

Kitty smiled. Sleeping was the last thing she was going to do!

Grandma read a story with Kitty, then pulled the curtains closed. 'Goodnight,' she said softly, and shut the door. Kitty listened to Grandma pottering about in the kitchen before eventually going into her own bedroom. Finally, the house was quiet.

Kitty threw back the covers, tiptoed downstairs, slipped outside and stood barefoot on the moonlit grass. She squinted, wishing her human eyes could see as well as her cat eyes. But even in the darkness, she could tell that Misty wasn't there. *She must have decided she's too frightened of Fang and Claws to come*, Kitty thought, feeling disappointed. *How will I find the Cat Council now?*

Then she heard a miaow from above her head. She looked up and saw a little cat perched in the oak tree. 'Misty!' she whispered happily. The silver tabby leapt down and landed lightly on the grass, rubbing her furry head around Kitty's ankles.

'Now I just need to turn into a cat!' whispered Kitty. She tried to remember exactly how it had happened last night. Her nose had been itching, and she'd sneezed …

'I'm going to need your help!' Kitty told Misty. She bent down close and buried her nose in the tabby's silky fur. Straight away, she could feel the itchy feeling in her nose and a noisy sneeze burst out of her. 'Aaaaaaa CHOOOO!'

Kitty crossed her fingers for luck and waited. She could feel the sparkling,

shimmering sensation spreading through her body again. She gave one more big sneeze – 'AAAAACHOOOO!' – and when she opened her eyes, she was whisker to whisker with Misty.

'It worked!' purred Misty.

Kitty looked around the garden. Everything looked clearer and every sound was sharper, from the rumble of Misty's purr to the *chirp-chirp* of a grasshopper on a nearby branch. Kitty swished her tail, twitched her whiskers and practised trotting around on her padded paws, getting used to being back in her cat form. 'Thanks, Misty!' she miaowed. 'I'm so glad you're here. I thought you weren't coming!'

'I was nervous about those horrid

Persians,' Misty admitted. 'I heard them prowling around. That's why I hid in the tree until you came outside!'

'We can't let them bully you, Misty,' Kitty told her friend firmly. 'You've been stuck inside all day because of those mean cats! Let's hope the Cat Council can help.'

'And tell us why you're turning into a cat too!' added Misty. 'Come on, let's go. I've never been to this Council's meeting place before, but we can use our noses to find the way.'

Kitty stared. 'Really?'

Misty raised her head and sniffed. Then she padded over to Kitty's Wendy house, jumped on to the roof and from there, leapt on to the garden fence. 'This way!'

Kitty followed cautiously. She wasn't sure she'd be able to jump on to the Wendy house roof – it seemed very high!

'Crouch low on all four legs,' Misty called encouragingly. 'Then spring up! It's easy.'

Kitty crouched, took a deep breath, then pushed off. She didn't jump quite high enough, and had to scrabble with her paws to get on to the roof – but she'd made it! Jumping on to the fence was easier. 'My legs feel so strong!' she miaowed, gazing around. 'And we're so high up. I can see into every garden on the street!'

'Now, use your claws to grip the fence, and your tail for balance,' Misty

explained, sniffing again to check they were going in the right direction.

'Slow down – I might fall!' said Kitty, carefully putting one paw in front of the other. But to her surprise, she could trot along just as quickly as Misty, her tail swaying from side to side. She followed Misty along the fence, on to a shed roof, and down an alleyway. They emerged in a patch of woodland that was full of bluebells.

'This must be it!' whispered Misty excitedly.

Kitty saw a group of cats sitting in a circle. As Kitty and Misty padded up to them, they turned to look at the newcomers. Kitty swallowed nervously. They had arrived at the Cat Council!

As Kitty and Misty got closer, some of the cats stepped aside to let them walk into the middle of the circle. *I've never seen so many cats together before!*

Kitty thought. There were silver tabbies like Misty; sleek gingers; tortoiseshells, fluffy greys with big blue eyes and even three kittens with fur the colour of honey.

The biggest cat was a tabby tom, who *miaow*ed sharply to get everyone's attention. *He must be the Guardian*, Kitty guessed. Then she noticed a small, dainty black cat with a white patch by her ear, her tail curled neatly around her paws. She was sitting quietly, but Kitty had a feeling she was important. Before Kitty could find out, the tabby tom made an announcement in a deep, serious voice.

'As our new members have arrived, it's time to open our meeting by saying the Miaow Vow,' he said.

Kitty listened in wonder as the cats recited what sounded like a poem.

'When you miaow,
We promise now,
This solemn vow,
To help somehow!'

Once the Vow was finished, the tabby padded forward. 'My name is Tiger,' he miaowed importantly.

'My human is Mr Thomas, on Beech Lane.'

Kitty's eyes went wide. 'That's my head teacher!' she whispered to Misty. 'I didn't know he had a cat.'

A plump, fluffy grey stepped up next. 'I'm Smoky,' she said in a friendly miaow. 'I love naps, sleeping and snoozing. It's nice to meet you.'

Another jet-black cat stepped forward. His green eyes were friendly, but he seemed shy. Kitty thought she'd seen him up on the hill in town, near her school. 'My name's Shadow,' he miaowed, and Kitty replied with a friendly miaow of her own.

As each cat introduced themselves, Kitty found herself purring happily alongside Misty. Now only the small black cat with the white patch was left. Kitty noticed the cat was wearing a collar that looked exactly like her own. 'Misty, look!' she whispered. But before she could say anything else, Tiger spoke again.

'Welcome to you both,' he began. 'I understand, from the scent message we found earlier today, that you called this Cat Council?' He nodded at Misty. 'Please, tell us how we can help.'

'Yes. My name is Misty, and I have a problem,' she explained. 'I love my new human, Jenny. But last night, I met two nasty cats in my garden. They chased me and my friend Kitty, and said they'd turn us into dog food!'

The gathered cats hissed at Misty's story, their whiskers shaking. 'Did they have fluffy, white fur?' a silky Siamese named Biscuits asked nervously.

'Yes!' replied Misty. 'Do you know them?'

'I'm afraid we do!' sighed Tiger. 'We've had problems with Fang and Claws for months. We've tried to give them a stern talking-to, but they just ignore us and after a while they're back to their old tricks!'

'Not long ago, they sneaked through my cat flap and ate all my special treats,' explained Biscuits sadly. 'They made a huge mess in the kitchen. My human got very cross and shouted at me!'

'They jumped into our garden when we were playing,' added one of the tiny honey-coloured kittens. 'We were so frightened that we hid in the shed!'

Tiger exchanged a glance with the small black cat with the white patch. 'Enough is enough. We're going to do everything we can to make sure that Fang and Claws stop this once and for all!'

Misty purred gratefully, then turned

to Kitty. 'My friend has something she needs to ask about too,' Misty said, nudging Kitty with her nose encouragingly.

Kitty looked around. 'Er, hello,' she said hesitantly. 'I'm Kitty. I hope you can help me. You see … I'm actually a girl. I turned into a cat last night, for the first time ever. And I don't know why!'

An excited murmur travelled through the circle. 'Another one!' breathed a little tortoiseshell next to Kitty.

'Well, you've come to the right place,' Tiger told Kitty solemnly. 'Our Guardian can help you.'

All the cats nodded respectfully as the small black cat with the white patch stepped quietly into the circle. *So she is the Guardian. I was right!* thought Kitty.

'Welcome, Kitty,' the Guardian miaowed. 'You have a very rare gift. The lucky humans who possess it can be wonderful friends to cats. In fact, I sense that you might even have what it takes to be our *new* Guardian.'

'*New* Guardian?' asked Smoky, puzzled. 'But what about—'

'I have decided to step down as Guardian of this Council,' the black cat explained. The other cats gasped. 'I am getting too old, but I had to wait until the right cat came along to take my place. Now, I believe she has.'

Misty purred, excited for Kitty. But the other cats seemed upset. 'B-but you've been our Guardian for years!' protested Biscuits. 'What will we do without you, Suki?'

Suki! thought Kitty. *That's the same name as —*

Suki held up a paw, and the circle

fell quiet again. 'I am sure Kitty will be an excellent Guardian,' she said. 'I know she is kind, thoughtful and brave, and will serve our Council well.'

'But *how* do you know that?' asked Tiger curiously. 'We've never met Kitty before.'

Suki's eyes twinkled. 'Because she's my granddaughter!' she announced proudly.

There were gasps around the circle. Kitty stared at the black cat in disbelief. *'Grandma?'*

Chapter 6

Finally, Kitty understood why Suki had a collar like hers. 'It's your necklace!' she exclaimed.

'I have waited a long time to tell you our secret,' Grandma miaowed happily. 'The females in our family have had this special ability for hundreds of years. I became a cat for the first time when I was your age, so I knew you were ready!

But you *must* keep it a secret, Kitty. If any human finds out about your gift, the magic will be broken, and you will never be able to turn into a cat again.'

'I understand,' Kitty replied solemnly.

Grandma purred proudly. 'Then you are on the right path to become our Cat Council's new Guardian!'

The rest of the circle had listened in silence, amazed. Now Kitty realised all the cats were purring together, a deep rumbling noise that she could almost feel in the grass under her paws. Grandma chuckled. 'I think the Council approves,' she whispered.

But something was bothering Kitty. 'I'd love to become the Guardian,' she said. 'The trouble is, I don't know how to help cats with their problems. I'm still getting used to being a cat myself!'

'You will learn,' Grandma reassured her. 'You just have to trust both your human and cat hearts, Kitty. Listen to them, and you will be a wonderful Guardian. I promise.'

Kitty thought of something else. 'Each time I've turned into a cat, it was because I sneezed! Could it happen when I don't mean it to? Is there an easier way?'

Grandma nodded at the charm on Kitty's collar. 'With practice, you will be able to turn into a cat and back whenever you want,' she explained. 'Just say the words.'

Kitty felt dazed. There was so much to remember!

'Now it's time to make your Guardian Promise,' Grandma told her. She held out her paw and asked Kitty to place her own paw on top. 'Kitty, do you promise to protect and help all cats, whenever you can?'

'I promise,' answered Kitty, feeling very serious.

'Then you may walk among catkind as one of them,' declared Grandma.

Suddenly Kitty was surrounded by the whole Council, all purring happily and wanting to bump heads with her. It felt strange at first, but Kitty quickly understood they were doing it to be friendly, and shyly bumped heads back. *I'm going to be the new Guardian!* she thought to herself, feeling a rush of amazed pride.

Misty was the last cat to rub heads with Kitty. 'Well done, Kitty!' she miaowed happily.

Grandma turned to Kitty. 'I think your first task in becoming the new Guardian should be to help your friend Misty,' she said. 'I'll help you if you need it. But I have faith that you can find a way to make it right.' She looked around the circle. 'If we don't stop Fang and Claws soon, they'll take over the whole town!'

Chapter 7

A day later, and Kitty's parents had arrived home that morning from their trip, bringing back lots of new things for their shop. But Mum and Dad were both tired from their long journey so, to Kitty's delight, they went to bed early that night. Grandma followed them upstairs, yawning loudly and winking at Kitty.

As soon as the house was quiet, she sprang out of bed and pushed her window open. She was going to try using the necklace to turn into a cat this time! Then she could go and see how Misty was getting on. Taking a deep breath, Kitty grasped the charm on her necklace, and quietly read the words on it:

'Human hands to kitten paws,

Human fingers, kitten claws.'

She closed her eyes as the tingling feeling shot through her body. When she opened them again, she'd turned back into a cat! And she hadn't even sneezed! Kitty felt pleased she was getting better at this, and she purred proudly. Then, with one easy leap, Kitty landed lightly on the window sill.

From here, she could jump down on to the kitchen roof, and then into the garden. She hesitated for a second, the breeze ruffling her fur. It looked like a long way, but she knew she could do it!

Once her paws hit the grass, she bounced straight on to the Wendy house, then padded along the fence until she reached Jenny's garden. Misty was peering nervously through the cat flap. As soon as she saw Kitty, she jumped through.

'I came as soon as my family went to bed!' miaowed Kitty. 'Any sign of Fang and Claws?'

Misty shook her head. 'No, thank goodness!' she replied – but as she spoke, Kitty felt her fur standing on end. She whirled round.

'I thought we told you this was *our* garden,' sneered Fang, his cruel eyes narrowed. Beside him, Claws hissed threateningly. The Persians had crept up behind Kitty and Misty without them noticing!

'Kitty, quick! Let's go back inside!' whispered Misty fearfully.

Kitty shook her head. 'You have to stand up to them,' she said under her breath. 'We can't let bullies get away with it.'

Misty looked a little unsure, but with another encouraging miaow from Kitty, she took a brave step forward. 'S-stop being so unkind,' Misty began. 'You have your own garden to play in!'

Claws prowled closer to them. 'Well, we want yours too,' he hissed. 'And you can't stop us!'

'That's where you're wrong,' Kitty said, moving to stand next to Misty.

'Misty has friends here in the neighbourhood. We won't let you push her around!' Kitty fluffed out her fur. She could sense Misty feeling more confident too.

'Yeah!' Misty added, looking Claws and Fang in the eyes. 'Why don't you just go back to your own garden?'

Fang looked puzzled, then surprised. He glared at Misty. 'Whatever, new cat. You just wait ...' he hissed, but then he finally turned and jumped up on to the fence. 'Come on, Claws,' he said, slinking away. Claws let out one more growl before following his brother.

'You did it!' said Kitty happily, bumping her head against Misty's. 'Well done!'

Misty purred gratefully. 'At least they're gone for now,' she said.

Kitty noticed movement on the fence. She saw a little black cat with a patch of white fur jump gracefully down into the garden.

'Well done, girls!' Bullies are always caught unaware when you stand up to them. Let's hope they don't come back.'

Kitty turned to her grandmother. 'Thanks, Grandma. What are you doing here?' she asked.

'I was just taking a midnight stroll. It's my favourite time to be a cat!' Grandma replied, trotting towards the garden gate. 'Why don't you and Misty join me on my walk, and I'll show you around?'

Kitty purred happily in agreement, and both she and Misty followed Grandma out of the gate, down a quiet alleyway and on to Willow Street, where Kitty's parents had their shop.

Kitty was excited to be spending time with Grandma as a cat, especially as Grandma pounced and ran through the streets!

'Keep up, kittens!' Grandma called, chuckling, as she raced along the top of a high wall.

As they padded along excitedly, Kitty noticed lots of curious, furry faces peering at them and smiling. 'Good evening!' Grandma called out to cats as they ran past. 'This is my granddaughter, Kitty, and her friend Misty, who's just moved to the neighbourhood!'

'It feels like every cat in the village must be out here, Grandma!' said Kitty, looking around. Cats were play-fighting in the street, and even snoozing in the moonlight. She recognised a few of them from the Cat Council.

'Almost!' replied Grandma. 'Cats love coming out at night when there are no humans around.'

Suddenly, Kitty felt something drip on her head. 'Oh, what's that?' she said, looking up.

Next to her, Misty let out a hiss. 'Rain!' she *miaow*ed, sounding alarmed. 'Quick! Get inside!'

Kitty giggled as all the cats began to race for cover, sheltering under trees and squeezing underneath cars. 'It's only a little shower,' she began. But when a second drop landed on her fur, she shuddered. 'Oh! But it feels horrid!' she exclaimed, surprised.

'Let's go home,' Grandma said, looking at the dark cloud gathering above them. 'It's going to pour. You'll soon find out there's nothing we cats hate more than getting wet!'

Kitty stared at Grandma. 'Cats hate getting wet,' she repeated. 'Grandma, you're a genius. You've just given me a brilliant idea. I think I know how to make Fang and Claws go away for good!'

Chapter 8

The next day was Saturday, and Kitty rang Jenny's doorbell after lunch. She and Grandma had searched their garden shed that morning, and found what they were looking for. Together, they'd carried the big cardboard box down the street to Jenny's house.

'Ooh, what's this?' asked Jenny's mum when she answered the door.

'My old paddling pool!' Kitty explained. 'Grandma and I wondered if Barney might like it? It's really good fun on a warm day!'

'That's so kind of you. I'm sure Barney will love it!' replied Jenny's mum. 'Why don't you come inside and we can set it up in the garden?'

Kitty caught Grandma's eye and winked. This was exactly what she had hoped for. Everything was going to plan so far!

Grandma left Kitty at Jenny's house, and her mum blew up the paddling pool and filled it with water. Jenny and Kitty giggled as Barney squealed and splashed water everywhere happily. 'He loves it!' said Kitty.

'I don't think Misty does, though,' said Jenny, pointing. Misty was curled up in a patch of sun at the other end of the garden, eyeing the paddling pool nervously.

'At least she's out in the garden today,' Kitty said, smiling at the little cat. *Because she knows Fang and Claws won't come back with people around!* she thought. *But if my plan works, Misty won't have to worry about those terrible cats any more.*

At the end of the afternoon, Jenny's mum lifted Barney out of the paddling pool and wrapped him in a fluffy towel. 'Time for dinner, then it's bedtime for this one!' she announced. 'Kitty, your grandma has just called to say your dinner will be ready in ten minutes, so you'd better get home. Thanks again for the paddling pool!'

'You're welcome!' replied Kitty, smiling.

Before she left, she nudged the paddling pool just a little further to the right. It had to be in the perfect spot for her plan to work – just underneath the fence …

After washing up that evening, it was time for Kitty to put the next part of her plan into action.

'I think I've left my book in the garden,' she told her dad. 'I'll just pop outside and look for it.'

'Good luck, Kitty-cat!' whispered

Grandma, as Kitty slipped out through the back door.

The sun had set, and the stars twinkled in a pretty violet-coloured sky. Making sure no one could see her, Kitty whispered the words on her necklace.

'Human hands to kitten paws,
Human fingers, kitten claws!'

As soon as Kitty had turned into a cat, she jumped on to the fence and ran along it until she reached Jenny's garden.

Misty was nowhere to be seen, and Kitty guessed that her friend was inside. She padded up to the cat flap, nudged it aside with her paw and miaowed, 'Misty?'

Misty was curled up on a kitchen chair. 'I have a plan. Come outside!' Kitty whispered.

Misty seemed nervous, and said that Claws and Fang had been out on the prowl earlier, but she jumped down from the chair and followed Kitty into the garden. Kitty explained her idea, but Misty was still not sure.

'Just remember how brave you were before,' Kitty said encouragingly. 'You can do it!'

Kitty hid behind a bush, and Misty waited on the lawn. Both of them listened out for any unusual noises. Soon, Kitty's ears twitched as she heard two fluffy tails swishing closer, and then two white faces popped over the fence, staring down at Misty. Even Kitty felt a bit worried as Fang gave a nasty, mocking laugh.

'We told you we'd be back when your friend wasn't around to protect you!' he hissed.

'Now we're going to take over your garden for *good*,' added Claws.

Kitty saw Misty take a deep breath. 'No, you're not,' she told the cats, shakily but firmly. 'This is *my* garden and *my* home!'

The Persians shot each other an amused glance. 'Oh, really?' miaowed Claws slyly.

'Really!' said Misty, taking another step towards the fence. 'If you don't go back to your own garden, you're going to regret it.'

Kitty felt so proud, especially knowing how scared Misty must be! She held her breath as the Persians arched their backs and bared their sharp teeth. She just hoped her plan would work! Just then, Fang hissed, 'Let's get her!' and he and Claws sprang down together ...

… and landed right in the paddling pool with a huge splash!

'Water!' spluttered Fang, gasping in horror. His fluffy white fur was dripping wet and plastered to his body. 'I HATE water!'

'It was a trap!' yowled Claws, scrambling out of the paddling pool. 'I don't want to come back to this garden any more, Fang!'

'Good!' shouted Misty, purring happily as the soggy cats ran away. 'That's what you get for being bullies!'

'That was brilliant! You were so brave, Misty,' said Kitty, rushing out from behind the bush and bumping heads happily with her friend. 'Well done!'

'Thank you so much for your clever plan, Kitty,' Misty replied. 'Just wait until we tell the Cat Council! You're going to be an amazing Guardian!'

'Let's go and tell Grandma it worked!' said Kitty excitedly.

Kitty and Misty trotted along the fence and jumped down into Kitty's garden. Kitty felt as though she might burst with pride.

'I'd better change back to a girl before anyone spots us,' she said to Misty.

Just as she finished reciting the magic words from her collar's charm, she heard Dad calling her name, and the back door opened. Dad and Grandma stepped outside together and Kitty saw a look of relief flash over Grandma's face when she saw that Kitty had changed back in time.

'Kitty!' said Dad in surprise. 'There you are! I was beginning to wonder what was taking so long. Did you find your book?'

'Err ... not yet,' answered Kitty. She looked down at Misty rubbing her furry head against her legs. 'I was just playing with Misty.'

'So this is Jenny's new cat! She's lovely, isn't she?' said Kitty's dad, bending down to stroke Misty, who purred happily. As her dad wasn't looking, Kitty flashed Grandma a big smile. *It worked!* she mouthed, and Grandma beamed back.

'Kitty, I've just realised something. You're not sneezing!' Dad exclaimed. 'Do you think you've grown out of your allergy?'

Kitty grinned. 'I must have!' she answered, tickling Misty under the chin. 'And I'm going to spend lots more time with cats from now on!' She couldn't wait!

Everyone thinks Shadow, the witch's cat, is scary.

Can Kitty use her magic to help him make friends?

Turn over to read some of Kitty's next adventure...

Kitty's magic
Shadow the Lonely Cat

Kitty and Jenny skipped ahead of Grandma, but as they turned the next corner, Kitty realised her friend was slowing down. 'What's wrong?' she asked.

Jenny pointed up ahead of them. 'Mrs Thornton's house is so spooky,' she said.

Kitty looked up the path lined with crooked old trees that led up to a big house at the top of a small, steep hill. The garden had a huge tree with twisted branches. It was full of tall, tangled, overgrown weeds, the black paint on the front door was peeling, and three of the windows were cracked. 'I know!' Kitty replied, shivering. 'My mum says she used to see Mrs Thornton doing shopping in town, but no one's seen her around recently. She's really old.'

'Some of the kids in our class say she's a witch,' added Jenny, eyeing the house nervously. 'She has a black cat called Shadow, and they say he's a witch's cat. Look – he's over there!'

Kitty caught a glimpse of wild dark fur and glinting eyes among the weeds. Shadow was crouched low, and Kitty could only just make him out. She remembered having met him once, but during all the nights she'd spent

wandering around town in her cat form, she hadn't bumped into Shadow since.

She tried to call him over, but Shadow turned away, darting through the bushes. Kitty saw the broken cat flap on the front door swinging as he rushed inside. *He obviously wants to stay close to home,* she thought.

After Kitty and Grandma had dropped Jenny off at home and walked along the street to their own house, Kitty decided to ask Grandma if she knew why she hadn't seen Shadow lately. After all, she was the perfect person to ask about any cat in town – because Kitty wasn't the only human who could turn into a cat. Grandma had the very same gift!

 # MEET

Kitty

Kitty is a little girl who can magically turn into a cat! She is the Guardian of the Cat Council

Tiger

Tiger is a big, brave tabby tom-cat. He is leader of the Cat Council

Suki is Kitty's grandmother. She can magically turn into a cat too!

Suki

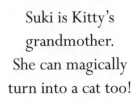

THE CATS

Misty

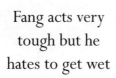

Misty is Kitty's best cat friend and loves to play with her ball of wool

Fang

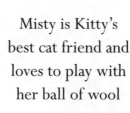

Fang acts very tough but he hates to get wet

Claws

Claws is Fang's twin brother. He is missing a chunk of his left ear!

FELINE FACTS

Here are some fun facts about our **purrrfect** animal friends that you might like to know ...

There are over **500 million** pet cats in the world!

Cats have **dreams**, just like people do

3.

Girl cats are called **'queens'** and boy cats are called **'toms'**

4.

Persian cats like **Fang** and **Claws** originated in Persia (modern-day Iran) over 500 years ago!

5.

A cat's night vision is **six times** more powerful than a human's